Window

Jeannie Baker

Puffin Books

I am grateful to Haydn Washington, biologist and environmental writer and consultant, for his help.

The artwork was prepared as collage constructions, which were reproduced in full color from photographs by David Cummings. The cover art was photographed by Murray Van Der Veer. The text type is Simoncini Garamond.

PUFFIN BOOKS
Published by the Penguin Group
Penguin Books USA Inc., 375 Hudson Street, New York, New York 10014, U.S.A.
Penguin Books Ltd, 27 Wrights Lane, London W8 5TZ, England
Penguin Books Australia Ltd, Ringwood, Victoria, Australia
Penguin Books Canada Ltd, 10 Alcorn Avenue, Toronto, Ontario, Canada M4V 3B2
Penguin Books (N.Z.) Ltd, 182–190 Wairau Road, Auckland 10, New Zealand

Penguin Books Ltd, Registered Offices: Harmondsworth, Middlesex, England

First published in the United States of America by Greenwillow Books,
a division of William Morrow & Company, Inc., 1991
Reprinted by arrangement with William Morrow & Company, Inc.
Published in Puffin Books, 1993

3 5 7 9 10 8 6 4

Copyright © Jeannie Baker, 1991
All rights reserved

Library of Congress Catalog Card Number: 92-62105
ISBN 0-14-054830-0

Printed in the United States of America

To Rodney, Haydn, and David

Happy Birthday
today you are

FRAGILE

FIRE
WOOD
SOLD HERE →

AUTHOR'S NOTE

We are changing the face of our world at an
alarming and an increasing pace.

From the present rates of destruction, we
can estimate that by the year 2020 no wilderness
will remain on our planet, outside that protected
in national parks and reserves.

By the same year 2020, a quarter of our present
plant and animal species will be extinct if we continue
at the current growing pace of change.

Already, at least two species become extinct each hour.

Our planet is changing before our eyes. However,
by understanding and changing the way we personally
affect the environment, we can make a difference.

JEANNIE BAKER was born in England and now lives in Australia. Since 1972 she has worked on her collage constructions, many of which are designed to illustrate picture books but stand individually as works of art. They are part of many public art collections and have been exhibited in galleries in London, New York, and throughout Australia.

Jeannie Baker is the author-artist of a number of distinguished picture books. Among them are *Home in the Sky*, an ALA Notable Book, and *Where the Forest Meets the Sea*, a *Boston Globe-Horn Book* Honor Book and the recipient of an IBBY Honor Award and a Friends of the Earth Award in Great Britain. *Where the Forest Meets the Sea* has also been made into an animated film directed by Ms. Baker.